Mr. Pam Pam AND THE HULLABAZOO

Trish Cooke

illustrated by
Patrice Aggs

CANDLEWICK PRESS
CAMBRIDGE, MASSACHUSETTS

Mr. Pam Pam comes to my house,

Mr. Pam Pam and the baby.

Mr. Pam Pam is so very tall—

his arms and legs are stringy.

He told me his favorite food

is banana ice cream with gravy.

One day right,
when Mr. Pam Pam came to visit,
I was watching TV.
Mom was playing music,
so we didn't hear the door until
Mr. Pam Pam lifted the flap
of the mail slot and started
shouting through it,

"PAM PAM KNOCKING
ON YOUR DOOR!"

and Mom went down to open it.

Mr. Pam Pam said,
"You'll never believe it,
but every word I say is true . . .

As I was walking over here
to come and see you
I saw a HULLABAZOO,
with yellow hands and
a green mustache!"

Mom laughed.

But me and
Mr. Pam Pam's
baby listened.
I've never seen
a Hullabazoo
before.

"And it bounced,
  and it bounced . . . "
  Mr. Pam Pam showed us.
  "And it twizzled
  and it twizzled
  till it could twizzle
  no more."

"Uh-huh,"
said Mom as she
stood by the door.
"And where is this
Hullabazoo now?"

And I rushed to the gate to see it too
because I'd never seen a Hullabazoo.

"Oh, it's gone now," said Mr. Pam Pam,
"but it was there when I saw it.
If you had hurried up
and opened the door . . .
maybe you would
have seen the
Hullabazoo too!"

Mr. Pam Pam comes to my house,

Mr. Pam Pam and the baby.

Sometimes he takes me to the park —

he lets me push the buggy.

But I can hardly reach the handles

and Mr. Pam Pam has to help me.

I like Mr. Pam Pam,

Mr. Pam Pam and the baby.

One day right,

when I was pushing the buggy,

Mr. Pam Pam shouted,

"WELL, GOODNESS GRACIOUS ME!"

I stood on my tiptoes
to try and see
what he could see,
but Mr. Pam Pam
ran on just a bit ahead
of me and pointed
around the corner.

He said, "You'll never
believe it, but every
word I say is true . . .
As I was walking just
a bit ahead of you,
I saw that Hullabazoo,
with yellow hands

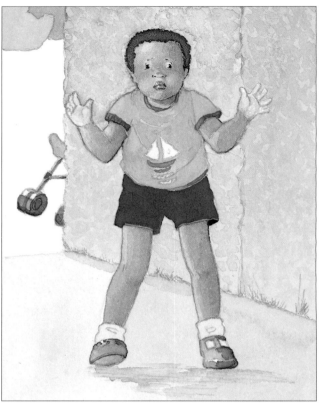

and a green mustache.
Its face was covered
with red and black dots,
and could you believe
that Hullabazoo
was wearing
purple socks!"

But when I got around
the corner . . .
that Hullabazoo
was gone.
I might have seen it
if I had run . . .

Mr. Pam Pam comes to my house,
Mr. Pam Pam and the baby.
He told me his favorite food
is banana ice cream with gravy.
So when he came yesterday
Mom made it specially,

but he said, "No, thank you — I've eaten already.
I had dinner with the Hullabazoo.
He's really quite friendly.
You'll like him too."

And in came the Hullabazoo,
with yellow hands and
a green mustache.
Mom laughed.
His face was covered
with red and black dots,

and the Hullabazoo
was wearing purple socks,
and a flat orange cap
with a star on the top.

And he bounced

and he twizzled—

A LOT,

A LOT!

And he said,

"I'm a Hullabazoo,
nice to meet you.
I'm a Hullabazoo!"

It's true . . .